PRESENTS
FRANKENSTEIN™

Adapted from the Universal film *Frankenstein*
by Mike Teitelbaum

Illustrated by Art Ruiz

Western Publishing Company, Inc., Racine, Wisconsin 53404

To Sheleigah, for watching the movie with me,
then reading each chapter as it took shape.
and
To A & C, for introducing me to the monster,
with a laugh.
—M.T.

Contents

CHAPTER 1
Night of the Grave Robbers

Dusk was falling, and the last rays of the flaming red sunset were disappearing. The darkness of the evening sky hung heavily over the stark brown and gray of the bleak mountains on the horizon.

A small funeral procession slowly made its way up a steep hill. The members of the procession were local peasants. They were carrying a dead man to the graveyard at the top of the hill. A priest led the way as four pallbearers carried the heavy coffin steadily up the incline, followed closely by the mourners.

A gravedigger was waiting patiently for the group at the hilltop cemetery. He had just tossed the last shovel of dirt from the grave onto a big pile of earth a few feet away.

The four pallbearers lowered the coffin into the fresh grave, their backs straining under their heavy burden.

Sobs of sadness turned into wails of despair as the mourners watched the simple wooden box disappear into the earth. The church bell continued to toll while the priest performed the service.

A few feet away Dr. Henry Frankenstein watched the procession from his hiding place behind a headstone. Next to him crouched his assistant, a craggy-faced, hunchbacked dwarf named Fritz. They heard only three sounds: the sad tolling of the church bell from the village at the base of the hill, the sobbing of the mourners, and the rhythmic chanting of the priest, who had just reached the top of the hill.

Soon, Dr. Frankenstein thought to himself anxiously. Soon.

Fritz slowly lifted his head above the top of the stone and stared out at the funeral with glaring eyes and a wicked smile.

"Down!" snarled Frankenstein in an excited, trembling whisper. "Down, you fool! They'll see you, and then all will be ruined!" Fritz obeyed his master, pulling his twisted face back behind the stone.

The short ceremony ended. One by one the mourners turned and started down the hill, followed by the priest. Only the gravedigger remained, to finish his work. He removed his jacket and spat on his hands, rubbing them together. Then he began to fill the grave with the loose dirt he had dug out earlier.

Once the coffin was covered and the grave filled in, the gravedigger patted the loose dirt on top with the back of his shovel. His work completed, he took his pick, his shovel, and his jacket, and started down the hill, moving slowly off into the night.

Frankenstein rose to his feet and watched the gravedigger disappear from sight. "Now, Fritz!" he demanded harshly. "Come on! Hurry! Hurry!"

The doctor grabbed two shovels and moved quickly toward the new grave, followed closely by Fritz. "Here, start digging!" he ordered. "The moon is rising! There is no time to lose!"

The two men worked quickly, shoveling the loose dirt out of the grave once again. Fritz clumsily dropped his shovel. It smacked against the side of the now-exposed coffin with a loud clang.

"Careful!" snapped Frankenstein, returning the hunchback's shovel to him.

Soon the digging was done. The two men lifted the coffin from the grave.

"Here he comes," cackled Fritz when he saw the long wooden box.

"He is just resting," Frankenstein said, more to himself than to Fritz, as he affectionately caressed the dirt-covered coffin. "Waiting for a new life to come!"

The two grave robbers loaded the coffin onto a large wooden handcart.

"Let's go, Fritz," ordered the doctor. They started down the hill, guiding the cart containing their stolen prize over the bumpy terrain.

The moon lit the sky as the two reached the main road at the bottom of the hill. After traveling a short distance, they came to a crossroads. Here, where the two paths met, they spotted a dead man swinging by his neck from a rope tied to a tree branch. A common criminal, left to public scorn, Dr. Frankenstein thought to himself.

"Look!" said Fritz excitedly, pointing to the body swinging in the night wind. "It's still here!"

Frankenstein let go of the cart handle, which dropped to the ground with a creaking thud.

"Climb up and cut the rope!" he commanded, pointing to the tree as he pulled out a knife.

"No!" grunted Fritz in fright.

"Go on," encouraged Frankenstein. "It can't hurt you! Here's a knife."

Holding the knife between his teeth, Fritz reluctantly began his climb up the tree. When he reached the branch that held the rope, he grasped the knife and called down, "Look out!"

The sharp blade easily sliced through the old rope, and the body dropped to the ground.

"Here's the knife," called Fritz, tossing it to the ground. "And here I come," he continued, scrambling down the tree to join Frankenstein.

The doctor, who was kneeling beside the body, gave it a quick examination, sighing deeply as he nervously rubbed his chin. He rocked back on his heels, then stood, pacing in the moonlight.

"Is it all right?" asked Fritz.

"The neck is broken!" said Frankenstein sharply. "The brain is useless now!"

Frankenstein grabbed Fritz by the shoulders and began to shake his frightened assistant.

"My work must go on!" he exclaimed in the voice of a madman. "We must find another brain!"

At a nearby university a class of medical students filed into a large amphitheater for that night's anatomy lecture. The young men and women slid into their seats, which were arranged in semicircles, row by row, up to the top of the lecture theater.

The students talked and joked quietly among themselves. Two lab assistants pulled a rubber cover over a body that had just been used for a dissection demonstration. A small wave of nervous laughter broke out when one of the assistants accidentally bumped into a skeleton hanging near the body. The skeleton bounced up and down on an elastic rope like a weird Halloween toy.

None of the students happened to glance toward the window at the back of the room. If they had, they would have seen the frightened, pathetic face of Fritz, peering into the classroom. Fritz glanced around the lecture hall, then ducked down out of view as the lecturer, Dr. Waldman, returned from a break in the class.

Dr. Waldman thanked his two assistants, who quickly left the room. He walked briskly to the lecture table. On this table sat two large covered glass jars. Each jar contained a human brain floating in a preserving fluid. Dr. Waldman waited for the class to settle down before continuing his lecture on the human brain.

"Ladies and gentlemen," he began, pointing to the jar on his right, "the normal brain. In this jar we have one of the most perfect specimens of the human brain ever to come to my attention here at the university."

Dr. Waldman then pointed to the jar on his left. "And here we have the abnormal brain of a typical criminal," he continued. "Observe, ladies and gentlemen, the scarcity of convolutions on the frontal lobes, as compared to those of the normal brain. Notice the distinct degeneration of the middle frontal lobe. All of these degenerate characteristics of the abnormal brain match perfectly with the history of the man to whom it belonged. His was a life of brutality, violence, and murder."

Dr. Waldman paused to let his words sink in and to give his students a moment to scribble in their notebooks.

"Both of these jars will remain here in the lecture

hall for further inspection," he concluded. "Thank you, ladies and gentlemen. That is all for tonight. The class is dismissed."

Dr. Waldman gathered his lecture notes and strode quickly from the classroom. His students collected their belongings and, still buzzing from the excitement of the night's lecture, shuffled from the room. Soon the lecture hall was empty.

This was what Fritz had been waiting for. When the last student had gone, he slowly opened the window and silently slipped into the lecture hall.

Fritz scurried across the room, keeping low to the floor. He paused for a moment at the operating table. A battle raged in his head. Although he was curious about the scientific wonders in the lecture hall, he was afraid he might get caught. He finally lifted the rubber sheet and took a peek at the dead body it covered. At his first glimpse of the cut-up cadaver, he dropped the sheet and let out a small grunt of horror. Then, his morbid curiosity satisfied, he proceeded with his mission.

He stared at the two jars containing the brains. Grabbing the jar with the normal brain, he turned to make his escape.

Suddenly a bell pealed loudly outside the window. Startled, Fritz dropped the jar containing the precious brain.

He stared at the mess on the floor. Shards of shattered glass mingled with fluid and splattered pieces of brain tissue. This brain was now useless.

"Urrr!" Fritz moaned in fear at the thought of the punishment awaiting him if he returned empty-handed to Dr. Frankenstein's lab.

Then he spied the other jar.

Smiling with relief, Fritz grabbed the jar containing the abnormal, criminal brain and moved back across the room. Carefully cradling the jar, he climbed out the open window, closing it behind him, and vanished into the night.

CHAPTER 2
The Doctor's Dreadful Experiment

A single large candle flickered in the ornately decorated parlor of the Frankenstein family villa. Its light reflected off the antique silver picture frame that sat on the hand-carved end table and contained a photograph of Dr. Henry Frankenstein.

The huge parlor was filled with family heirlooms. A large wooden mantel was prominent in the high-ceilinged room. Fine oil paintings adorned the walls, and priceless oriental rugs covered the hardwood floor.

Dr. Frankenstein's fiancée, Elizabeth, was staying at the Frankenstein villa in order to prepare for her forthcoming wedding to Henry. The blond-haired beauty now paced nervously over the fine rugs, clutching a letter tightly in her fist. The letter was from Henry, and its contents were quite upsetting.

This was not the first time Elizabeth had ever worried about Henry. More than once in the past he had stayed away for weeks at a time, lost in his research. But not like this. Never quite like this. There was something about this letter that made her shudder. It almost sounded as if someone else had written it, someone strange and evil.

Suddenly the door to the parlor swung open and a maid announced a visitor. "Mr. Victor Moritz to see you, miss," said the servant.

Elizabeth practically ran across the room to greet her guest. "Victor, I'm so glad you've come," she said, extending both her hands in greeting. She was relieved to see him.

Victor Moritz immediately saw the frightened look in Elizabeth's eyes as he grasped her hands, thrilled to be in her presence again.

Victor was Henry Frankenstein's best friend. It was this fact, as well as his strong sense of loyalty, that forced him to bury his true feelings for Elizabeth. Deep in his heart Victor knew that his affection for her was more than simple friendship. But he could never admit that to Elizabeth. After all, she was engaged to marry his best friend.

"What is it, Elizabeth?" he asked, concerned.

Elizabeth, unable to speak, bowed her head and walked anxiously across the room.

Then Victor, following her, spotted the letter in her hand.

"It's Henry!" he cried. "You've heard from Henry!"

Elizabeth nodded nervously. When her words finally came, they came swiftly.

"Yes!" she exclaimed, shaking the letter in her fist. "It's the first word I've had in four months. It just arrived. He's never stayed away so long." She looked straight into Victor's eyes. "Oh, Victor, you must help me!" she pleaded desperately.

Victor touched her arm for a fleeting moment. "Of course I'll help you!" he said, trying to sound comforting.

Elizabeth covered his hand with her own. For one brief second their eyes met. Then she moved quickly back across the room. "I'm frightened, Victor!" she cried, growing more agitated as she spoke. "I've read this over and over again, but I just don't understand it. Listen."

With trembling hands Elizabeth unfolded the crumpled letter and held it close to her eyes, which grew moist with tears. Sighing heavily, she chose a random passage from Henry's letter and read it out loud:

"'You must have faith in me, Elizabeth, and wait. My work must come first, even before you.'"

Elizabeth's voice cracked as she looked at Victor through tear-filled eyes. She took a deep breath, then read on:

"'At night the wind howls in the mountains. Prying

eyes can't peer into my secret. I am free to work with interference from no one.'"

"What can he mean?" Elizabeth asked, hoping Victor could shed some light on the mysterious letter.

"I don't know," muttered Victor. "What else does he say?"

"'I am living in an abandoned old watchtower, close to the town of Goldstadt. Only my assistant is here to help me with my experiments—'"

"Oh, his experiments!" interrupted Victor.

"Yes," said Elizabeth, lowering the letter as she looked up at Victor with red-rimmed eyes. "That's what frightens me. The very day we announced our engagement he told me of his . . . his . . ." She could barely bring herself to speak the word. ". . . his experiments!" she spat out bitterly, beginning to cry again.

"He said he was on the verge of a discovery so terrifying that he doubted his own sanity!" Elizabeth continued. "There was a strange look in his eyes that day. Some . . . mystery. His words carried me away, as they always do. You know how charming Henry can be. Of course, I've never doubted him, but still I worry. I can't help it! And now this letter, I—" She shook her head, leaving the sentence hanging.

Elizabeth crossed the room, lowering her head to hide her tears. "Oh, this can't go on!" she finally blurted out. "I must know what is happening to him!"

Victor wanted to take Elizabeth in his arms and offer her the comfort she so obviously needed. But he resisted this urge and instead stood silently before her. Elizabeth, regaining her composure, finally spoke again.

"Victor, have you seen Henry in the past few months?" she asked.

"Yes," he responded. "About three weeks ago. I met him walking alone in the woods. He spoke to me of his work, too. I asked if I might visit his laboratory. He just glared at me and said he would let no one go there. His manner was indeed very strange."

"What can we do?" Elizabeth cried frantically. "Oh, if he should be ill!"

"Please don't worry, Elizabeth," said Victor calmly. "I will go to Dr. Waldman, Henry's old professor at the medical school. Perhaps he can tell me more about all this."

"Victor, you're a dear," sighed Elizabeth gratefully, putting her hand on the lapel of his coat. It was an innocent gesture, but it affected Victor nonetheless.

"You know I would go to the ends of the earth for you, Elizabeth," said Victor quietly, the tenderness in his voice unmistakable.

A flicker of a smile crossed Elizabeth's face. "I shouldn't like that," she said. "I am far too fond of you already."

"I only wish you were," said Victor warmly. He

longed to reveal his deep feelings to her, but instead he said nothing. Nevertheless, his hand reached for hers, almost unconsciously.

Elizabeth drew her hand away quickly and bowed her head. "Victor," she said compassionately, not wanting to hurt this man who was now helping her in her time of need.

Victor's face hardened. The moment had passed.

"I'm sorry," he said stiffly, then turned and walked toward the door to leave.

"Good night, Victor," Elizabeth said softly, feeling strangely sad. "And thank you. Thank you!" She rushed past Victor and opened the door for him, holding it as he slipped out into the hall.

"Good night," said Victor, turning to face her. "And don't worry! Promise?"

"I promise," she answered, smiling.

Elizabeth hesitated at the door, then dashed out into the hall.

"Victor!" she called, catching up to him.

"What is it?" he asked.

"I'm coming with you!" she stated firmly.

Victor raised his hand and shook his head in protest. "But, Elizabeth, you can't do that!" he cried.

"I must!" she insisted. "I'll be ready in a minute." She rushed up the stairs.

Victor sighed, then waited for her in the hallway.

Dr. Waldman's study looked very much the way Elizabeth thought it would look. Floor-to-ceiling bookcases lined the large room. These were filled with handsome leather-bound medical volumes and the doctor's personal files. But there was something a bit more unusual displayed on the shelves: rows of stark white skulls, evidence of the years Dr. Waldman had spent studying the human brain. Elizabeth tried not to shudder as she and Victor took seats at the huge oak desk across from the doctor.

Waldman's face was lit by a tall oil lamp that stood next to him on his desk. His keen brown eyes revealed the wisdom he had gained during his many years of practicing medicine.

Having learned a great deal from Dr. Waldman, his mentor, Henry Frankenstein had grown impatient. He felt that Waldman was unadventurous, unwilling to plunge headlong into the unknown region where science and philosophy met. Dr. Waldman, however, felt that Henry had delusions of grandeur and that these delusions had no place in the world of a dedicated scientist. The two had finally parted ways a few months earlier.

Now Waldman leaned across his desk. Looking at Elizabeth and Victor, he began to speak.

"Henry Frankenstein is a brilliant young man," he

explained. "But he is also erratic and unscientific at times. He troubles me."

"I'm worried about Henry," Elizabeth said nervously. "Why did he leave the university? He was doing so well. And he seemed so happy with his work."

Waldman remained silent for a moment. Then he folded his hands together and looked directly at Elizabeth. "Dr. Frankenstein's research in the field of chemical galvanism and electrobiology is far ahead of our theories here at the university. In fact, they have reached a most advanced stage. They have become dangerous."

Waldman was quite fond of Henry Frankenstein. Henry had been his best student, and he regretted their parting. He also worried that Henry's dreams of power might take him to the edge of madness.

"Dr. Frankenstein is greatly changed," Waldman stated.

Victor spoke for the first time. "You mean he has changed as a result of his work?" he asked.

"Yes, his work," Waldman nodded, growing disturbed. "His insane ambition to create life!"

Elizabeth turned pale. "How?" she cried. "How? Please tell us everything, whatever it is!"

Waldman hesitated, then shifted in his seat and began an incredible story:

"Henry told me that the bodies we now use for lecture and dissection purposes weren't perfect enough for his experiments. He wanted us to supply him with other bodies, fresher bodies, and we were not to be too particular as to where and how we got them. I told him that his demands were unreasonable, and so he left the university in order to work unhampered. He found what he needed elsewhere."

Victor and Elizabeth were stunned by Waldman's words. Elizabeth could hardly believe the doctor was speaking about the same Henry she knew.

"Oh, you mean he took the bodies of animals," said Victor, trying to collect himself and sound casual. "Well, what are the lives of a few animals?"

Waldman shook his head and turned slowly around to face Victor. His lips were drawn tightly over his teeth, for he was trying to keep his impatience in check. He chose his words carefully.

"You do not quite get what I mean," the doctor said deliberately. "Dr. Frankenstein is only interested in human life! He wants to destroy it and then re-create it! There you have his mad dream!"

A heavy silence descended on the office as the weight of Dr. Waldman's words sank in. Elizabeth got up from her chair, holding the back of her hand to her forehead. She walked across the study floor, then turned sharply.

"Can we go to him?" she asked desperately.

"You will not be very welcome!" Waldman responded curtly.

Elizabeth shrugged, her despair growing. "What does that matter?" she asked in a quivering voice. "I must see him. Dr. Waldman, Henry respects you. Won't you come with us?"

Waldman stared at her for a long time. "I'm sorry," he said gently. "Dr. Frankenstein is no longer my pupil."

"Please," cried Elizabeth, "won't you help us bring him home?"

Waldman wavered for a few moments. Finally his affection for Henry won out over his memory of their disagreement. "Very well," sighed the doctor. "I've warned you. Still, if you want me to go, I will!"

Dr. Waldman rose from his chair, grabbed his coat, and followed Victor and Elizabeth outside. They hailed a carriage and headed toward the town of Goldstadt.

CHAPTER 3

Terror in the Tower

A distant shaft of lightning illuminated the night sky, silhouetting a centuries-old watchtower. The tower's ancient stones glistened in the torrential rain, which blew sideways in sheets before cascading down the tall structure.

The watchtower stood near the crest of a mountain just outside the town of Goldstadt. It appeared ghostlike, desolate and abandoned. The tower's roof had been reconstructed so that half of it slid open, providing access to the recently established laboratory below.

Dr. Frankenstein's assistant, Fritz, scurried around the roof, fighting the blinding rain. He worked quickly, connecting wires that ran up from the lab to a huge antenna that rose above the roof and searched the stormy sky for lightning.

Lightning. Henry Frankenstein knew this was the

key. The life-giving power of natural electricity had been ignored by Waldman and the other fools at the university. But after tonight the entire world would know.

Frankenstein was dressed in a white surgical suit. He worked feverishly in the laboratory that had been set up in the tower's main room and was now filled with electrical equipment. The room's high ceiling and vast stone walls dwarfed the scientist as he worked.

"Fritz!" he called up through the open roof.

"Hello!" came the response as Fritz leaned over and stared down at his master in the lab far below.

"Have you finished making those connections?" Frankenstein shouted.

"Yes!" Fritz shouted back, nodding his head. "They're done!"

Thunder rumbled in the distance. The fiercest part of the storm was still some thirty minutes away.

"Well, come down, then!" Frankenstein snapped. "Come help me with these attachments. We've no time to lose and lots to do."

Fritz scrambled down a rope as Frankenstein mixed a chemical solution in a tall glass vial. When Fritz reached the floor of the lab, he tried to assist Frankenstein. His efforts were futile, however, for the doctor was in a highly nervous state. Fritz eventually shrank back, hoping to stay out of his master's way.

A flash of strange, unearthly lightning and a rumble

of thunder, louder than before, frightened Fritz. He dropped to the floor near Frankenstein's feet, trembling in terror.

"Fool!" sneered Frankenstein, making no effort to hide his contempt for the hunchback. "If the storm develops as I think it will, you'll have plenty to be afraid of before this night is over!"

Frankenstein began adjusting the equipment on the tower wall. "Attach the electrodes!" he ordered, moving from one piece of apparatus to the next. His surgeon's gown was stained with chemicals, and his haggard face looked as if he had not slept in days. He placed his stethoscope against a piece of delicate electrical equipment as if it were a human patient and listened carefully.

"Oh, it will be magnificent!" he said softly, a smile of satisfaction lighting up his weary face. "This storm, the lightning, all the secrets of the heavens!"

He turned to Fritz. "And this time we are ready, eh, Fritz?" But then, noticing a look of horror on Fritz's face, he asked, "What's the matter?"

Fritz pointed to a long steel surgical table, which sat on the floor of the lab, directly below the opening in the roof. On this table, covered from head to toe with a shimmering metallic cloth, lay a huge figure. This was the body Dr. Frankenstein had created, sewn together from the dead body parts he and Fritz had stolen in recent weeks. This was the creature Frankenstein was determined to bring to life this very evening. All of his efforts would at last bear results.

In an almost fatherly manner Frankenstein took Fritz by the hand and led him to the table. He lifted the cloth that covered the body, revealing the monster's arm. "See, Fritz," began Frankenstein. "There's nothing to fear. No blood, no decay. Just a few stitches. Look!" He caressed the dead arm lovingly, fondling the sutures that held the hand to the wrist.

"And here," Frankenstein continued, "the final touch." He slowly folded the cloth back from the creature's head. "The brain you stole, Fritz!"

"Yes!" said Fritz, smiling proudly now.

"Think of it," said Frankenstein, his voice rising in triumph. "The brain of a dead man, ready to function again in a body I made with my own hands!" He held his hands in front of his face, staring at them. Then he gently re-covered the creature's head with the cloth.

Suddenly his mood changed, and he turned to Fritz. "Throw the switches!" he barked. "Let's have one final test!"

Fritz obeyed, scampering from machine to machine, throwing the power switches.

Electrical equipment sparked to life. Small jagged bolts of power danced from one electrode to the next. Dials whirled, readings on indicator meters leapt off the scale, and the lab itself became a living thing.

Outside, the thunder crashed even louder than before. The storm was moving closer.

"Good!" exclaimed Frankenstein. "When the storm is at its height, we'll be ready. Fritz, turn everything off for now. I must—"

He was interrupted by a pounding at the door.

"What's that?" he hissed, listening intently. The pounding at the door came again.

"There's someone out there," muttered Fritz, moving toward the stairs that led down to the front door.

The hollow, knocking sound echoed up the stairs, this time louder, more insistent.

"Go!" Frankenstein commanded Fritz. "Send them away! No one must come in here!" His panic rising, Frankenstein shoved his assistant toward the stairs. "Go, Fritz! Quickly! Send whoever it is away!"

Fritz, lantern in hand, hurried down the twisting, shadowy stairs. "Who would be coming around at this time of night?" he muttered to himself, shuffling along, step by step. "There's too much to do!"

The knocking continued, agitating the already nervous assistant. "Wait a minute!" he shouted at the door. "All right! I'm coming! I'm coming!"

Fritz reached the large oak front door and flung open the viewing panel. A rain-drenched face pressed up against the outside opening.

"It's Dr. Waldman, Fritz!" the professor shouted.

"You can't see him," snarled Fritz. "Go away!" He slammed the panel shut and started back up the stairs, more agitated than ever.

Outside, Elizabeth, Victor, and Dr. Waldman pressed against the wall of the tower, seeking some shelter from the increasing downpour.

"Henry!" shouted Victor as Waldman resumed his furious pounding.

"Henry!" echoed Elizabeth. "Open the door!"

"Frankenstein!" added Waldman. "Let us in!"

Back in the lab Frankenstein rushed to the upstairs balcony and peered down. "Who is it?" he shouted, nearly mad with rage. Then, not waiting for a response, he added, "Leave me alone! What do you want?"

Elizabeth looked up through the driving rain to the small balcony above. "Henry!" she called. "It's Elizabeth! Open the door!"

Henry's tone softened as he met her gaze. "What do you want?" he cried. "Please, give me time! You must leave me alone!" He turned and dashed back into the lab.

In a pitiful voice Elizabeth called up to him once more. "Henry, at least give us shelter!"

This was more than Frankenstein could stand. He bounded down the stone stairs and threw open the front door. Elizabeth and the other soaked visitors entered the tower's hallway.

"Henry!" she cried warmly, rushing to him.

Frankenstein stepped away from her, moving backward up the stairs. "Elizabeth, please," he pleaded. "Won't you go away? Trust me, just for tonight?"

"I trust you," Elizabeth said soothingly. "I believe in you, but I can't leave you tonight."

"You've got to leave!" ordered Frankenstein, his face twitching.

"You're inhuman!" shouted Victor as Frankenstein's gaze darted wildly around the hallway. "And you're crazy!"

This word seemed to trigger a change in Frankenstein. His eyes widened, and his lips stiffened. He spoke in a cool, challenging voice.

"Crazy, am I?" he began. "All right, we'll see if I'm crazy or not!" He gestured for the others to follow him. "Come with me!" He turned and started up the stairs.

The others followed, frightened by Henry's sudden change of mood but eager to finally learn what was going on. When they reached the laboratory door, Frankenstein put his hand on the knob and paused.

"Are you quite sure you want to come in?" he asked, facing the others.

All three visitors nodded.

"Very well," said Frankenstein. He opened the door and stepped into the lab. When everyone was inside, he quickly shut the door and locked it.

"A moment ago you said I was crazy," he began as soon as they were seated, looking particularly at Victor. "Tomorrow we'll see about that." Then he turned to Dr. Waldman.

"I learned a great deal from you at the university, Doctor," he said, leaning toward him. "All about the violet ray and the ultraviolet ray, which you said was the highest color of the spectrum. You were wrong!"

Frankenstein paused and pointed to the equipment all around him. "Here, with this machinery," he continued, "I have gone beyond that. I have discovered the great ray that first brought life into the world!"

"Oh?" responded Waldman skeptically. "And what is your proof?"

"You shall have your proof tonight, Doctor," answered Frankenstein, smiling. "At first I experimented only with dead animals; with them I got a slight flicker of life. Then I kept a human heart beating for three weeks. But now I am going to turn this ray of life onto this body." He paused, pointing to the huge creature on the operating table. Then his voice rang out, "And I intend to give it life!"

"You really believe you can bring the dead to life?" asked Waldman in a shocked tone.

"This body is not dead!" Frankenstein exclaimed, growing more excited with each word. "It has never lived! I created it, pieced it together with parts of bodies taken from graves and gallows. Go, Doctor. See for yourself!"

Waldman gave Frankenstein a doubtful look, then walked over to the operating table. He pulled back the cover and examined the creature, only to discover that Frankenstein had been telling the truth. Feeling faint, he returned to his seat.

Frankenstein moved to the table and leaned against it, his back to the body, his arms spread wide, as if protecting it.

Outside, lightning flashed and thunder clapped at precisely the same second. The storm was directly overhead.

"Ah, the overture begins," stated Frankenstein. Ignoring the visitors, he turned to his assistant. "Fritz! Is everything ready? Let's move!"

Fritz sprang into action, charging up power supplies and completing last-minute connections. Frankenstein himself moved quickly, fine-tuning the equipment and making adjustments in power levels. The massive electrical machines sprang to life, sparks flying. Small bursts of energy leapt from electrode to electrode.

Frankenstein and Fritz moved to the body. They pulled back the cover, then prepared the table to be lifted up into the night sky. Frankenstein grabbed the wheel controlling the pulley system. While Fritz kept an eye on the electrical readings, Frankenstein turned the wheel, sending the table straight up toward the opening in the roof. Higher and higher it went. Light flashed above it from the sky, and electricity from the wires leading to the body crackled all around it.

The table cleared the opening, and then it was outside, above the tower's roof. Lightning struck the lifeless creature several times. Below, Frankenstein stared up, his eyes glittering with exhilaration. The others huddled together in terror, not quite believing what they were witnessing.

When the body had been outside long enough, Frankenstein turned the control wheel in the opposite direction and lowered the table back down to the lab floor. He rushed to the creature's side as Fritz turned off the machinery.

There, on that stainless-steel operating table, was the gruesome result of his many months of hard labor. The creature's hand quivered with life, the fingers moving as if grasping for something solid to hold.

Waldman, Fritz, and Frankenstein stooped over the twitching creation while Victor tended to Elizabeth, who had passed out.

"It's moving!" shouted Frankenstein, laughing madly. "It's alive! Alive!" he cried, delirious with joy and exhaustion.

Victor rushed to his side. "Henry!" he shrieked, horrified at his friend's condition. "In the name of God!"

"God?" muttered Frankenstein. He turned to Victor and in his madness exclaimed, "Now I know how it feels to be God!"

As thunder continued to crash outside, Victor and Waldman held Frankenstein up, for he was in danger of collapsing. Elizabeth, now conscious, buried her face in her hands and wept.

CHAPTER 4
Alive!

Victor and Elizabeth returned to the Frankenstein villa that same night. Dr. Waldman remained at the watchtower to care for Henry and to help him with the follow-up to his experiments.

Elizabeth was haunted by her memories of that night, for she could not forget the crazed look in Henry's eyes. She only hoped that all of this madness would soon be left behind, and that she and Henry would be together again.

The following morning, however, she and Victor had a more immediate problem. Henry's father, Baron Frankenstein, was a stubborn old man; quite powerful and respected in the village, he was used to getting his own way. Elizabeth and Victor now sat across from him in the parlor, attempting to convince him that his son was all right. This was proving to be a difficult task.

"Henry is well, but he is very busy," began Victor, trying to sound convincing. "He promised to get in touch with you soon. Try to be patient for just a little longer, Baron."

"Please don't worry about him," added Elizabeth, longing to forget about the horrors of the previous night. "He'll be home in a few days."

The Baron stared at them. "You two have it all figured out, don't you?" he said, making no effort to hide his annoyance. "You think I'm an idiot! Well, I'm not! Anybody with half an eye can tell there's something wrong. Come on, what is it?"

"You are quite mistaken, Baron!" said Victor, shaking his head.

"Bah!" grumbled the Baron. "Tell me what my son is up to!"

"He is completing his experiments," said Elizabeth, smiling in order to conceal her own concern. "That's all."

"But why is he working in a ruined old tower when he has a decent house, good food, and a darn pretty woman right here?" the Baron asked suspiciously.

"Baron, you don't understand," sighed Elizabeth.

"I understand perfectly well," said the Baron. "It's another woman. I'm sure of it."

"Oh, you're wrong!" cried Elizabeth.

The group was interrupted by the arrival of the mayor of the village, known as the Burgomaster by the locals. The Baron made no secret of his intense dislike for this man.

"Good day, Baron," said the Burgomaster cheerfully. Then he turned to Elizabeth. "Madam," he said, bowing courteously.

"What do you want?" growled the Baron in his most unfriendly voice. "If it's trouble, we've got plenty of that already!"

"Oh, there's no trouble, sir," answered the Burgomaster quickly.

"What do you mean, no trouble!" barked the Baron. "There's plenty of trouble!"

"Well, sir, what I . . . that is . . ." The Burgomaster stumbled over his words in confusion. "When will the wedding be, if you please?" he finally asked.

"Unless Henry comes to his senses," the Baron blurted out, raising his voice, "there'll be no wedding!"

"But, Baron, the village is all prepared," the Burgomaster protested. "Everything is ready for the big celebration!"

This was more than the Baron could stand. "Don't you think I know that, you idiot!" he shouted.

The Burgomaster, not wanting to be insulted, prepared to leave. "Good day, Baron," he said politely, but through clenched teeth.

"Good riddance to you," the Baron shot back.

The Burgomaster turned on his heel and stormed from the room.

"Well, there you are," the Baron said, turning back to

Victor and Elizabeth. "The whole village is kept waiting, the bride is kept waiting, and I am kept waiting. Henry is coming home, if I have to bring him back myself!"

"No, Baron," Victor began, but his words were futile. The stubborn Baron Frankenstein had made up his mind. He was going to bring his son home.

A few days later Frankenstein was still in the tower. He had spent much of that time trying to catch up on his sleep. But he'd also spent many hours making careful notes on the work he had done. Now he sat at a desk, watching Dr. Waldman pace nervously around the lab.

"Oh, come and sit down, Doctor," said Frankenstein calmly. "You must be patient. You can't expect perfection at once!"

"This creature of yours should be kept under guard!" stated Waldman firmly. "Mark my words, he will prove dangerous!"

"Dangerous?" said Frankenstein, astounded at the doctor's fear. "Haven't you ever done anything dangerous? Where would we be if no one wanted to explore the secrets that lie beyond our present knowledge? If no one ever wondered what causes trees to bud, or what changes darkness into light? If I could discover just one of those things—what eternity is, for example—I wouldn't care if they thought I was mad!"

"You are young, my friend," said Waldman patiently.

"Your success has intoxicated you. Look at the facts. This fiend's brain—"

"It's a perfectly good brain, Doctor," said Frankenstein, interrupting Waldman. "You ought to know: It was taken from the amphitheater!"

Waldman's face grew tense. "The brain that was stolen from the amphitheater was a criminal brain!"

Frankenstein looked over his shoulder at Fritz. Stupid, hopeless Fritz, he thought. What a foolish blunder! This would be dealt with later.

Frankenstein turned back to Waldman and defended his work. "Oh, well," he said as casually as possible. "It's only a piece of dead tissue."

"It is a criminal brain," Waldman shot back. "Only evil can come of it! You have created a monster!"

"I have faith in this 'monster,' as you call it," argued Frankenstein.

"Think of Elizabeth," countered Waldman, "and your father!"

Frankenstein's expression darkened, and his voice grew soft. "Elizabeth believes in me. My father has never believed in anyone! My creation is only a few days old. I've got to experiment further. It's—"

Frankenstein was cut off by a strange sound coming from behind a wooden door across the room. It sounded like the whimpering of a frightened animal.

"Here it comes!" said Frankenstein. The two men

moved toward the large oak door, which swung open slowly.

A hideously grotesque figure stood in the door frame. The inhuman creation towered more than seven feet tall. It wore an old suit, far too small for it. On the wrists that stuck out beyond the sleeves could be seen the stitches that held the hands in place. The top of the head was flat, like the lid of a box. A repulsive scar ran the length of the creature's forehead, evidence of the seam that had been closed after the stolen brain was placed in its skull.

Waldman backed away in horror, but Frankenstein slowly moved toward the monster.

"Come in," said Frankenstein gently, as if speaking to a small child. "Come in."

The monster came forward, sliding its feet along the floor, moving on joints still too stiff to bend. Its head stooped low, and its arms hung limply at its sides.

"Sit down!" ordered Frankenstein, pointing to a chair. "Sit down!" he said, louder now.

Walking jerkily, the monster slowly made its way to the chair and sat down.

"You see!" Frankenstein shouted triumphantly to Waldman. "It understands! Watch!"

Frankenstein ran to the wheel that controlled the roof door and slid it open. Sunlight poured down on the monster. It slowly raised its head to investigate the strange sensation of light and warmth, experiencing both for the first time. It seemed to like this new feeling and raised its arms toward the light.

Frankenstein moved toward his creation.

"Take care, Henry!" called Waldman, still quite frightened of the creature. "Shut out the light. We don't want to get it agitated."

Frankenstein closed the roof door, then stood before the monster, who lowered its head and arms. It now held out its hand to Henry, like a child reaching out for a parent.

"Sit down," said Henry gently. The monster took its seat, but its hands still trembled. It seemed touched and confused by the sunlight.

"It understands!" Henry repeated, overjoyed at his apparent success.

Suddenly Fritz came running into the room, carrying a flaming torch. "Dr. Frankenstein, Dr. Frankenstein! Where is it? It's gotten away. It's— Ahhh!"

Fritz had been asleep. When he awoke and discovered the monster gone, he had panicked. Now, upon seeing the creature out with the doctors, he shrieked and waved the burning torch at the equally panicked beast.

The monster stood, whimpering in fear, waving its hands at the torch, trying to make it go away.

"You fool!" scolded Frankenstein. "Can't you see it's afraid of the fire? Take that torch away!"

But it was too late. The monster was terrified. Fritz,

now terrified himself, ignored his master's orders and continued to wave the flaming torch at the cowering brute.

The monster struck out, knocking the torch from the dwarf's hand, then easily shoved him away. Frankenstein grabbed the creature, but it had tremendous strength and effortlessly knocked its creator to the ground.

"Shoot it!" shouted Waldman, his worst fears confirmed. "It's a monster!" Waldman grabbed a large wooden board and smashed Frankenstein's creation on the back of the head. The creature groaned and fell to the ground, unconscious.

Frankenstein scrambled to his feet, shouting. "Get some rope, quickly!"

The three men bound the monster's hands and feet. "Let's take it to the cellar," Frankenstein ordered. "We'll put it in chains!"

The three men dragged the heavy brute away.

Down in the tower's cellar, the monster rocked its enormous body back and forth, struggling in vain to break the chains that bound it. Its pitiful howls echoed off the stone walls as it waved its shackled arms above its head.

The loud wails brought Fritz into the cellar. "Quiet!" yelled the dwarf, cracking a whip at the monster's feet. "Quiet!"

Fritz hated this thing. It terrified him, for he had seen its awesome strength.

But Fritz enjoyed exercising power over this creature. Having been a servant his whole life, he was finally in a position to command something inferior to himself. He was now relishing, even abusing, the authority Frankenstein had given him.

The monster's cries brought Frankenstein running into the room. When he saw how Fritz was tormenting the poor, chained creature, he pulled him away.

"Stop that howling!" Frankenstein shouted at the monster. "The whole countryside will be upon us!" Then he turned to Fritz and screamed, "Leave it alone, you fool! It's got the strength of ten men! Give me that whip!"

Fritz reluctantly dropped the whip.

"That's enough, Fritz," Frankenstein commanded. "Leave it alone!" And he stumbled out the cellar door, grasping his head in despair.

When his master was no longer in view, Fritz continued harassing the creature, this time shoving the dreaded torch at the hulking brute.

The monster retreated into a corner, shrinking away from the flame and growling at Fritz. It dropped fearfully to the floor, rolling from side to side on its back and resuming its pitiful wailing.

The monster now felt passionate hatred for Fritz. This was a new feeling it had learned. It wanted only to be free of its chains so that it could kill this loathsome dwarf.

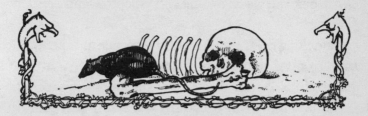

CHAPTER 5
The Monster Strikes Back

Frankenstein and Waldman spent the next few days writing and organizing notes from the experiment. Although Frankenstein was beginning to lose hope for the long-term success of his work, he never mentioned this to Waldman.

One evening, while the two doctors were working in the lab, they suddenly heard a tortured, bloodcurdling shriek coming from the cellar.

"What was that?" wondered Waldman, moving to the door.

A second piercing scream, louder than the first, sent both men running from the room.

"It's Fritz!" cried Frankenstein as he led the way down the stairs to the cellar.

As they approached the heavy cellar door, they heard a satisfied grunt coming from the other side.

"Come on, Doctor! Quickly!" shouted Frankenstein. "Hurry!"

He flung open the door and stepped into the room, then stopped immediately, stunned by the sight that greeted him. Across the dank cellar the lifeless form of Fritz dangled from a chain, his neck grotesquely stretched, his limp body swinging back and forth.

"Fritz!" gasped Frankenstein, nearly fainting from the shock. "The monster has killed Fritz!"

A low, growling sound cut through the dark cellar. The monster stepped from the shadows, free of its chains, one of which had formed Fritz's makeshift noose.

"Look out!" cried Waldman, pulling Henry back through the doorway.

The monster moved with surprising speed. Waldman tried to slam the cellar door, but the monster was too fast for him. Its snarling face and clawing hands stuck through the opening.

"Henry!" shouted Waldman, trying to rouse his startled friend. "We've got to get this door closed. If it gets out, we're both doomed!"

Frankenstein regained his senses just in time to add his strength to Waldman's. Together they managed to shove the monster back. Then they slammed the door and bolted it shut.

The creature, once again trapped, pounded at the door, howling for freedom. Frankenstein, leaning against the stairway wall for support, lowered himself to the steps.

"It always hated Fritz," Frankenstein whined, placing his head on his hands, surprised at the sadness he felt at the death of his assistant. "Fritz always teased it, tormented it, but I never thought the creature was capable of this!"

"Come, come," said Waldman sharply. "Pull yourself together! We've got to deal with that . . . that thing in there!"

"What can we do?" asked Frankenstein, shrugging hopelessly, still terribly shaken.

"Kill it!" snapped Waldman, taking charge. "As quickly as possible! But first we must overpower it. Get me a hypodermic needle!"

"You're talking about murder!" cried Frankenstein, unwilling to destroy his creation even now.

"It's our only chance!" countered Waldman savagely, running out of patience. "In a few minutes it will get through the door! Hurry!"

The monster continued pounding furiously on the door. Waldman could hear the rusty, ancient hinges creaking under the tremendous strain. Frankenstein flew up the stairs, heading back to the lab. He returned moments later, holding a loaded syringe. "Here it is," said Frankenstein, handing the needle to Waldman.

"Good," replied Waldman. "Now stand there near

the door. As soon as it moves toward you, I'll stick the injection in its back."

They stepped up to the door, Waldman holding the needle, Frankenstein brandishing a flaming torch.

"Ready?" asked Waldman.

"Yes," sighed Frankenstein, not fully convinced this was the right thing to do, but too drained to argue.

Frankenstein reached for the bolt and started to unlock the door. Just then, the door flew open, revealing the snarling, panting form of the monster.

The enraged creature rushed at Frankenstein, who thrust the burning torch at the towering brute. But the monster had learned quickly. It ignored the dreaded fire and moved forward, knocking the torch from Frankenstein's hand.

As its massive hands closed around Frankenstein's throat, it began choking the man who had given it life. The creature seemed to be enjoying this ghastly work.

Waldman dashed from his hiding place behind the open door and jabbed the hypodermic needle into the monster's back. The beast, surprised by the needle's stabbing pain, let out a groan and released its grip on Frankenstein's throat. It knocked Waldman to the floor, then turned back toward Frankenstein, who was down on one knee, gasping for breath.

Once again the monster's hands closed around Frankenstein's throat. It flexed its powerful muscles, preparing to crush the doctor's windpipe. Suddenly the creature's eyes glazed over, and it loosened its death grip. The injection had taken effect. The creature whimpered in confusion as it stumbled, hands trembling, then crashed to the floor beside Frankenstein.

Frankenstein rushed to Waldman's side. "Dr. Waldman, are you hurt?" he asked hoarsely, for his neck was sore from the creature's choke hold.

"No, I'm all right," responded Waldman, getting to his feet.

They heard a knock at the front door. Oh, will this never end? thought Frankenstein.

"Go see who's there," said Waldman as he attempted to straighten his rumpled clothes.

Frankenstein grabbed the flaming torch and ran to the door. It was Victor.

"Henry, what's going on?" Victor cried when he spotted the monster's motionless body on the floor. "Elizabeth and your father are coming up the mountain to see you!"

"You must stop them, Victor!" said Frankenstein, panic rising within him.

"It's too late," said Victor, shaking his head.

Waldman, realizing the seriousness of their situation, sprang into action. "They mustn't see this," he said, leaning over the monster. "Here, give me a hand, both of you."

The three men dragged the creature's huge body into the cellar.

"Henry," Waldman ordered, "hurry upstairs and clean yourself up. Your father and Elizabeth will be here any minute."

Clutching his aching head, Frankenstein stumbled up the stairs.

At that very moment the Baron and Elizabeth turned onto the path leading to the tower's front door.

"Queer sort of place for a son of mine to be in, I must say," sneered the Baron when they reached the door. "I don't like it at all. But here goes!"

The Baron rapped the door with his cane. There was only silence within. "There doesn't seem to be anybody in the place," he grumbled impatiently.

Just then Victor opened the door, out of breath, his clothes a mess.

"What's the matter with you?" asked the Baron, pushing past him into the tower. "You look as if you've been kicked by a horse! Where's Henry?"

"Uh . . . um . . . that is . . ." stammered Victor, totally at a loss for words.

"Well?" pressed the Baron irritably.

"He can't be disturbed just now," Victor blurted out hastily.

"Oh, can't he?" snapped the Baron. He was used to getting whatever he wanted. "Well, I'll soon settle that

FRANKENSTEIN™

Pull-out Poster From Spine

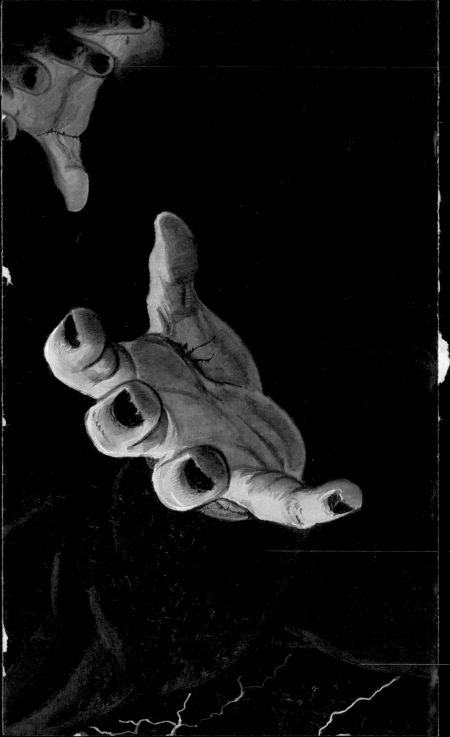

nonsense!" He rushed past Victor and began looking around.

Then Elizabeth spoke up. "Victor, where is he?"

As Victor gestured with his head, indicating the upstairs lab, Waldman hurried into the hallway, straightening his tie and smoothing his hair into place.

"Who the devil are you?" barked the Baron.

"I beg your pardon, sir," replied Waldman with as much dignity as he could muster. "I am Dr. Waldman."

"Oh, are you?" responded the Baron. "Well, I am Baron Frankenstein. Perhaps you know what all this nonsense is about, because I certainly don't!"

"I suggest you take Henry away from here at once," counseled Waldman gravely.

"What do you think I've come for?" said the Baron, exasperated. "Come, Elizabeth, let's see what's going on."

Elizabeth helped the Baron up the winding stone stairs that led to the lab. She knew it wasn't going to be pleasant for Henry to face his father's wrath. But she could think of no way to stop the old Baron. Besides, she too was concerned for Henry, and deep in her heart she agreed with the Baron that Henry should return home at once.

Elizabeth knocked timidly on the lab door. "Henry?" she called softly.

"Come in," came the weak answer from within.

Elizabeth threw open the door and found Frankenstein lying on a sofa, totally exhausted and on the verge of collapse.

"Henry!" she cried, almost bursting into tears at the sight of him.

"Elizabeth," he muttered lovingly, trying to stand. He rose to his feet, extending his arms, then collapsing on the floor in front of her.

"Victor! Dr. Waldman! Come quickly!" Elizabeth shouted, rushing to Henry's side. "Oh, my dear, what has happened to you?"

The Baron entered the lab, followed closely by Victor and Waldman, who had run up the stairs at Elizabeth's cry.

"Get him onto the sofa," ordered the Baron, taking charge. The three men lifted Frankenstein and placed him back on the sofa. "Have you got any brandy in this place?" asked the Baron, his love for his son replacing his earlier annoyance.

Dr. Waldman rushed to a cabinet across the room. "Hurry up!" the Baron shouted. "Here, I'll take that," he said as Waldman returned with a glass of brandy. He and Elizabeth lifted Frankenstein's head off the sofa. "Henry, my boy," the Baron said quite gently, "drink this!"

Frankenstein opened his eyes and stared up at his father, who tilted the glass toward his mouth.

"There, that's better," said the Baron. "I'm going to

take you home with me, Henry." Baron Frankenstein spoke in a comforting tone, one the others had not heard him use before.

"No! I can't go," said Frankenstein, sitting up, growing more disturbed as he spoke. "What about my work? And what will happen to my notes, the records of my experiments?"

"I will see that they are preserved," replied Waldman, touching Henry's arm gently.

Henry suddenly remembered the creature he had created and began to panic. He looked at Waldman. "But what of the—"

"I'll see that it is painlessly destroyed," Waldman said quickly, before Henry could reveal the monster's existence to his father.

"No!" protested Henry. But arguing made him tired again, and he sank back into the sofa cushions.

"You just leave it all to me," said Waldman.

"Poor Fritz," moaned Frankenstein feebly. "It's all my fault."

"You can't do anything more now, Henry," said Elizabeth softly. "You must come home so you can get strong again. You'll feel better as soon as you get out of here."

Frankenstein sighed weakly, trying to accept the apparent end of his great experiment.

CHAPTER 6
From the Tower . . .

From outside, the tower appeared dark and deserted. But a look inside Henry Frankenstein's laboratory would reveal that it was inhabited by two individuals—Dr. Waldman and the hideous creature Frankenstein had created. The monster was stretched out on an operating table in the middle of the room. A sheet covered all but its gruesome head and one arm, which hung out from beneath the sheet like a dead limb on a dying tree. The monster was unconscious, having received numerous injections from Dr. Waldman.

Waldman sat at a desk covered with papers, charts, and notebooks, all documenting the experiments—the horrors as well as the successes—of the past few months.

Before Frankenstein left the tower, Waldman had promised to preserve the records of his experiments. This had proved to be a more tedious task than

Waldman had anticipated. Being a man of his word, however, the doctor had kept his promise. His work was now nearly complete.

But there was one other thing Waldman had promised Henry: He had vowed to destroy the monster!

The doctor now moved across the room toward the operating table. The last injection he had given the creature contained a massive dose of poison, but even that had not done the job.

Waldman lifted the monster's enormous arm and found a faint pulse. Then he examined the misshapen head. Satisfied, the doctor went back to the desk, opened a large journal, and began to write:

"Note increased resistance to poison, requiring stronger and more frequent doses. Will perform dissection at once. Remove the brain. Kill it, once and for all."

Across the room, as the doctor made his entry in the journal, the monster stirred. Its eyelids fluttered open, then closed again.

Waldman shut the journal and carried a small case of surgical instruments over to a wheeled cart, which was covered by a white cloth. He laid the sharp steel instruments on top of this cloth, preparing for what he believed would be the final chapter in the story of this ghastly experiment.

An icy chill ran down his spine as he remembered everything that had taken place here in this room. Let's get this cursed thing over with quickly, he thought, and then get the devil out of this sinister place forever.

The doctor donned his surgical gloves and wheeled the cart over to the operating table, placing it up near the monster's head. He leaned over the hulking brute and pressed his stethoscope against its chest, his face turned away from the monster's face.

The creature's eyes opened again. This time they remained open. It looked up at the back of Waldman's head, then slowly raised its arm. Its huge hand grabbed the back of Waldman's neck.

The doctor let out a strangled grunt as he struggled in vain against the monster's incredible strength.

The monster sat upright on the table, its grip on Waldman remaining firm. Then its other hand closed around Waldman's throat. The doctor let out a last, helpless gasp.

Finally Waldman was still. As the monster loosened its grip, the doctor's lifeless body slumped to the floor.

The monster stumbled down the stairs leading from the lab, its back bent, its legs stiff, its long arms swinging limply at its sides.

At the bottom of the stairs it looked around, confused, grunting and growling like a caged animal.

Then it found the tower's front door and flung it open. Still groggy from the poison, it staggered outside.

In the gardens at the Frankenstein family villa, Henry and Elizabeth clinked their glasses together, then sipped fine champagne.

Henry had been home for several days now, and a newfound peace could be seen in his face. The happy couple sat on comfortable lounges in the lush garden, enjoying the tranquillity of a perfect afternoon.

"It's like heaven being with you again, Elizabeth," Henry said softly.

"Heaven wasn't so far away all that time, you know," replied Elizabeth with a smile.

"I know, my dear," said Henry, taking her hand. "But I didn't realize it at the time. Through all those horrible days and nights, I could think of nothing but my work!"

"Henry," she interrupted with a gentle shake of her head. "You must forget about those things. You promised!"

"All right," he sighed, leaning his head toward hers and pushing away dark thoughts. "Let's talk about us! When shall our wedding be?"

"Oh, let's have it soon, my love!" Elizabeth replied. She was relieved to have Henry back, safe from that dreadful place. She let the warm feeling of her love wash over her as she moved closer to him.

"We shall have the wedding as soon as you like," said Henry, gazing at her. He had forgotten how beautiful she was. He had been a fool to stay away so long.

In the distance a church bell rang out, its deep peals lingering in the air. Elizabeth tilted her head up toward Henry's face. As she closed her eyes, Henry leaned down and gently caressed her hair. Then their lips met in a loving kiss.

On the day of Henry and Elizabeth's wedding, the Baron threw a huge party to celebrate the joyous occasion. He provided food and drink for the whole town, as he wanted all of the local villagers to participate. The Frankensteins were the most powerful and influential family in the region, and a wedding in their house was a holiday for the whole town. Groups of merrymakers gathered in the streets surrounding the villa. Musicians played their flutes and accordions, while the townsfolk danced and sang. Flags waved gaily in the soft breeze, and flowers decorated every home. Sounds of laughter and celebration mingled with the chiming church bells. A festive, carnival-like atmosphere filled the air.

The Frankenstein parlor, which looked out onto the joyous scene, was decorated for the party taking place inside. Streamers hung from the central chandelier, extending out to all corners of the huge room.

Baron Frankenstein stood before a small table draped with fine linen. On the table, under a glass bell, several Frankenstein family heirlooms were arranged. In the center was a wreath of silk orange blossoms against a backdrop of faded blue velvet. On each side of the wreath sat a small velvet flower. Inside the wreath was an oval picture frame containing a photograph of the Baron as a young man in his formal wedding suit, standing by his bride, Henry's dear, departed mother.

Now the Baron stood with Henry, Victor, and many other party guests. Elizabeth was still in her bedroom with the bridesmaids, getting ready for the ceremony. The crowded room grew quiet when the Baron lifted the glass bell that protected the precious family treasures.

"For three generations this wreath of orange blossoms has been worn by the bride at our family's weddings," the Baron began. All eyes in the room watched him as he picked up one of the flowers.

"Your great-grandfather wore this, Henry," he continued, placing the velvet boutonniere into the buttonhole of his son's jacket. "But it looks as good as new now!"

Frankenstein nodded at his father, a gesture of thanks and appreciation. The Baron picked up the other boutonniere.

"And here's one to make the best man look still better!" said the Baron, placing the second flower on Victor's lapel.

"Thank you, sir," responded Victor, honored to be a part of this great family tradition.

The Baron lifted the orange blossom wreath and

handed it to Henry. "Thirty years ago I placed this on your mother's head," the Baron explained. "And today you'll make me very happy by doing the same for Elizabeth! And I hope, in some thirty years' time, a son of yours will continue this tradition."

A cheer rose from the guests.

"And now," continued the Baron, "how about a toast?" The butler brought in an old bottle of wine, which he carried on a spectacular silver tray.

The butler poured wine for the guests. Then the Baron raised his glass and said, "Here's a wish for a happy marriage—and a long life for Henry and Elizabeth!"

"Long life!" cheered the guests in the room.

Shouts could be heard coming through the window that led out to the balcony. "Good health to the bride and groom!" cried the villagers outside.

Victor went to the balcony and looked down on the festive crowd. "They're calling for you, Baron!" he shouted across the room.

"Well, I suppose I'd better show myself," said the Baron, moving toward the window. As he stepped out onto the balcony, a joyful roar rose from the happy throng.

"Thank you all very much!" the Baron cried. "I'm very pleased to see you all! I hope you have enough food and drink, and I hope you all have a wonderful time. But it looks as if you're enjoying yourselves already!"

The crowd cheered and waved at the Baron, who slipped back into the parlor to attend to his guests. Outside, the party continued. Church bells rang as the townspeople danced and sang in the streets—men, women, and children, all celebrating this wedding in the House of Frankenstein.

CHAPTER 7
Maria and the Monster

The monster ran through the woods, crushing brambles beneath its gigantic feet and using its powerful arms to force its way through the thick bushes and trees. It had been wandering aimlessly for hours, wanting only to get as far away as possible—far away from the tower and the horrors it had seen there.

The creature was confused and filled with strange sensations: hunger, exhaustion, loneliness. It had no words for these basic human perceptions, which this creature was experiencing now for the first time.

As it neared a small clearing by a lake, the monster heard voices. It paused, cautious and fearful of humans, who had always treated it with cruelty. Parting the branches of a tree, the monster gazed upon a picturesque scene.

A modest but attractive cabin stood near the shore.

On the other side of the lake, beautiful mountains rose majestically, their images reflected in the water. Sunlight sparkled off the lake's calm surface like polished diamonds.

In the front yard of the cabin, a villager was sawing wood, sweating as he worked in the brilliant sunshine. He was a middle-aged man of average height and weight. Nearby, his little daughter played with a tiny kitten.

"Stay here, Maria," her father said, putting down his saw and wiping the sweat from his forehead with his shirt-sleeve. "I'm going to have a look at my traps. Then we'll go into the village and join the big wedding celebration, okay?"

He walked over to Maria and hugged her. She was his pride and joy. Things had been hard for the two of them ever since his wife died. Maria was so young, and there was so much work to do around their homestead. But he loved the child, and she loved him. Somehow they had been getting by.

"You won't be long, Daddy, will you?" she called as he started to leave.

"Oh, no, sweetheart," he said warmly. "I'll be back in a flash."

"Daddy," said Maria, "won't you stay and play with me for a little while?" She never seemed to get enough of her father's time.

"I've got too much to do, Maria," he replied, feeling a bit guilty, as he always did when he had to leave her.

"Stay and play with the little kitten, okay?" He leaned over and kissed her head. Then he headed off, away from the lake.

"Good-bye, Daddy," called Maria, waving.

"Good-bye!" he called back. "You be a good girl now!" Then he turned and disappeared from her view.

"Come on, kitty," said Maria, by now used to amusing herself while her father attended to his chores. She wandered down to the edge of the lake, petting her kitten and looking out on the glorious view.

The monster crouched in the bushes, staring at Maria. It had never seen a child before. This little one, who held an even smaller creature in her arms, made the monster curious, though a little wary. It stood now, drawing itself up to its full height, then moved slowly forward.

The huge creature stepped from the woods, and Maria's eyes opened wide at the sight of it. The immense, ungainly figure took several steps toward her, then stopped. Maria was surprised and confused. She hadn't heard this very large man approach. She wondered where he had come from.

"Who are you?" she asked in her friendliest voice. When she got no response, Maria put the kitty down and walked over to the big stranger.

It gazed down at her, a look of wonder in its eyes.

The child looked up at the weird-looking man and smiled. "I'm Maria," she said, introducing herself.

The monster continued to stare at her with the same odd expression on its face. It wasn't afraid of the little one; it had just never learned to trust anyone or anything in its short, miserable existence.

Maria, on the other hand, had never had a reason to distrust adults, even if they did look rather strange. Although she was puzzled by the man's silence, she needed a companion. "Will you play with me?" she asked, smiling. When the strange man failed to respond, she took its mammoth hand and led her new playmate down to the edge of the lake.

The monster was willing to be led by this little one, for it found the lake's surface, with the sun shimmering upon it, fascinating.

Maria bent down and started to pick some of the daisies growing wild along the shoreline. She brought the flowers up to her nose, inhaling deeply. Delighted by their sweet fragrance, she turned to her new friend. "Would you like one of my flowers?" she asked, selecting a daisy and extending her hand.

The monster's eyes dropped from Maria's face to the flower she held in her hand. Its expression changed slowly, softening. A smile spread across its face as it extended its hand to take the flower. Then it held the flower and grunted happily. No one had ever behaved kindly toward it before.

Maria laughed and ran closer to the lake's shore. She

continued picking flowers, happy that she had made this strange man laugh.

The monster followed her. When it reached her side, it dropped down to its knees to be closer to her level.

"You can have these flowers," she said, handing a few more daisies to the creature. "And I'll keep these!"

The monster laughed and handed some of the flowers back to her.

"I can make a boat!" exclaimed Maria. "Watch!" She chose one of her flowers and tossed it into the lake. The daisy floated on the surface, bobbing up and down on the little swells that lapped gently at the shore.

"See how mine floats!" she said to the big man. "Now you try one!"

The monster watched as she threw another flower into the water. Then it took one of the daisies and clumsily tossed it into the lake. The monster laughed with delight at this activity, for it had learned its first game. It beamed now with a childlike wonder. This little girl made the creature feel good, not hurt or frightened or angry like the other humans it had known.

Maria tossed the last of her flowers into the lake. The monster, carried away with joy, threw its entire handful of flowers in as well. Then it looked down at its empty hands. A puzzled expression came over its face, followed by one of concern. The creature liked this game, but it did not know how to make it continue.

It looked up at the little one and smiled. It had discovered a way to keep the game going. It stood up and walked over to her. Stooping down, it picked the little one up in its arms.

The monster was very strong, and its powerful grip hurt and frightened Maria. "No!" she shouted. "Stop it, you're hurting me!"

The creature did not understand. It took two steps toward the shore, then, kneeling, tossed the little one out into the lake. A smile crossed its face. It fully expected this friend to float, just as the flowers had done.

Maria thrashed about in the water, trying in vain to swim. As she struggled, she tried to cry out, but her lungs filled with water. Then she sank beneath the lake's surface for the final time.

The monster panicked. It stood, waving its hands frantically, as if this might bring the little one back. Then, throwing back its head in grief, it let out a mournful cry. The creature was filled with pain, and for the first time in its life, it felt sadness.

It turned and ran back and forth along the shoreline. Then, sensing it might be discovered if it remained where it was, the monster ran back into the woods, trying, as it stomped through the brush, to run away from this new-found pain.

CHAPTER 8
To the Villa

Back in the village the wedding party continued on the streets. Sounds of laughter and violins filled the air. Women in long skirts and men in short pants and feathered hats kept time to the music, dancing the very same dances that had been done for generations.

The sound of this merriment drifted up through the balcony window into Baron Frankenstein's parlor, where his guests were also enjoying themselves, celebrating the forthcoming wedding of Henry and Elizabeth.

Elizabeth quietly entered the parlor in her magnificent wedding gown. The gown was made of white satin, with lace sleeves sweeping down to a point over the backs of her slim hands. Her long embroidered veil, pushed back from her face, was held on by a white skullcap decorated with flowers.

Tradition usually deemed it bad luck for a groom to

see his bride before the ceremony on the day of the wedding. Elizabeth, however, overwhelmed by a strange feeling of dread, broke with that custom now and cried out to Henry, who was chatting with some party guests near the parlor balcony.

"Henry!" she called in a soft voice that did not hide her distress.

Henry turned at once, pleased to see her, but surprised that she would walk into this room full of guests, allowing all, including him, to see her before the big moment.

"Elizabeth!" he called back, moving across the room and taking her hand. "How lovely you look!" He gazed into her eyes. "But you really shouldn't be here. It's bad luck, you know."

"I must see you for a moment," she replied. She held his hand tightly, closing her eyes.

"Why, Elizabeth, what's the matter?" he cried.

Elizabeth motioned toward the door. Henry followed her out of the parlor, through several connecting rooms, and into her bedroom.

The room was filled with Elizabeth's bridesmaids, who were gaily chattering about the upcoming ceremony. They stopped talking, though, when they saw Henry, shocked by the groom's unexpected appearance.

"Could you leave us for a moment?" Elizabeth asked the bridesmaids.

"Why, of course," replied her maid of honor, leading the other young women from the room. When the last bridesmaid had closed the bedroom door behind her, Henry turned to Elizabeth.

"Now, my darling, what is it?" he asked, concerned.

Elizabeth stood silently for a moment, her eyes downcast. Then she looked up at Henry. "Oh, I'm so glad you're safe!" she cried.

"Safe?" Henry replied with a puzzled frown. "Of course I'm safe." Staring straight into Elizabeth's eyes, he grasped her hands and continued, "You look so worried, dear. Is anything wrong?"

"No," she began hesitantly, unable to look straight into his eyes. "Forgive my foolishness, Henry! It was just a mood. Nothing is really the matter."

"Of course not, dear," said Henry, wanting to believe her, but confused by her obvious distress.

Elizabeth hesitated, wondering why she was afraid to tell Henry the truth. That was, after all, the reason she had brought him into this room. She had to tell him!

"Henry, I'm afraid!" she blurted out with sudden passion, her voice intense, her eyes looking deeply into his. "Terribly afraid!"

"Oh, Elizabeth!" Henry replied, shocked by her sudden flood of intense emotion.

"Where is Dr. Waldman?" she continued. "Why is he late for the wedding?"

"Don't worry," Henry said, "he's always late. He'll be here soon." He noticed a faraway look in her eyes and began to worry.

"Something is going to happen," Elizabeth continued. "I can feel it. I can't get these terrible thoughts out of my mind!"

"You're just overly excited," said Henry tenderly, trying to convince himself as well as Elizabeth that his words were true. "It's the wedding and all the preparations that have gone into it. Of course you're nervous!"

"No, it isn't that," she said quickly, shaking her head. "I've felt it all day. Something is coming between us. I know it!" She buried her head in her hands and began to tremble.

Henry took her gently by the shoulders and tried to lead her to a chair. "Sit down," he pleaded. "Rest a bit. You look so tired!"

Elizabeth slipped away from him, ignoring his advice. "If only I could do something to stop it, to save us!" she cried, becoming more upset.

"From what, Elizabeth? From what?" asked Henry, not understanding her alarm.

"I don't know!" she replied anxiously. "If only I could get it out of my mind." She took a deep breath, then grabbed Henry's arm, clutching it tightly. "I'd die if I lost you now!"

"You'll never lose me!" Henry responded.

"Are you so sure?" she asked, turning away, her voice suddenly flat and emotionless. She paused. Then her words became passionate once again. "Oh, I love you so!" she cried, rushing into Henry's arms.

"You know I love you, too!" said Henry, trying to comfort her.

"Oh, Henry, I—"

Elizabeth was interrupted by an insistent knock on the door.

"Who's that?" she asked nervously.

The knock came again.

"Henry, open up!" cried a voice from the other side of the door.

Henry rushed to the door and flung it open. Victor, looking as white as a ghost, stood before them, quivering in shock.

"Henry," he said in a trembling voice. "It's Dr. Waldman!"

Victor spoke softly, for he did not want Elizabeth to hear what he was saying. His words reached her ears, however, and she became hysterical.

"I knew it!" she screamed. "I knew something terrible was going to happen!"

"Victor, tell me," said Henry urgently, "what has happened to Waldman?"

Victor looked at Elizabeth, who was sitting on the edge of her bed, wringing her hands anxiously. He motioned for Henry to step out of the room. As Henry started to follow Victor, Elizabeth stopped him.

"Henry!" she cried. "Don't go! Don't leave me!"

"Please, darling," said Henry, moving away, "stay here."

Henry and Victor left the room, closing the door behind them. Henry took a key from his pocket and locked Elizabeth's door from the outside. She struggled with the doorknob, calling to Henry, but her efforts were useless. She was trapped in her room.

"Dr. Waldman has been murdered!" Victor informed Henry once the door had been locked. "They found him in the watchtower—strangled to death!"

"It's the monster!" whispered Henry, suddenly overcome with guilt. First Fritz, now Waldman. He felt responsible for both horrible tragedies.

Victor nodded grimly. "Yes, the monster," he repeated. "It's been seen in the woods. The people in that area are terrified. Some of them have said—"

Victor was cut off by a sinister, unearthly howl echoing through the house.

"It's here!" cried Frankenstein, every nerve in his body tingling with fear. "It's in the house!"

A second menacing howl filled the hallway.

"It's upstairs!" shouted Frankenstein. "Come on!"

Henry and Victor rushed to the stairs. As they ran off, Elizabeth pounded on the door to her bedroom. "Henry!

Henry!" she cried desperately. But Henry and Victor were gone.

The two friends bounded up the stairs and searched the upper part of the villa. But they found nothing.

"It's got to be here somewhere!" shouted Frankenstein. "We heard—"

At that moment there was another roar.

"What fools we were!" cried Frankenstein. "It's down in the cellar!"

They turned and ran back down the stairs.

Meanwhile Elizabeth paced back and forth in her room. Occasionally she would pause and put her ear to the door, desperate to know what was happening.

She was able to pick up bits and pieces of conversation. She knew something terrible had happened to Dr. Waldman. But there was something else, something evil. What had sent Henry and Victor running off? She had to know what it was. Was Henry in danger? Oh, why did all of this have to happen—and on their wedding day, no less? She sank into an overstuffed chair, resting her head on her hands.

Behind her, across the room, the monster's face appeared at the window. Peering in, it spied Elizabeth. Its powerful fingers lifted the window, and its huge form squeezed into the room.

Elizabeth, unaware of the monster's presence, got up from her chair and returned to the door. She pulled on the knob in frustration, but the lock held firm. Henry, wanting only to protect her, had locked her in! She was trapped, stuck in this room until someone came to let her out.

The monster slowly approached her, its bulky, clumsy body surprisingly quiet as it moved. When it was almost upon her, it let out a chilling growl.

Elizabeth, shocked by this ominous sound, turned around. Unable to utter a word, she looked at the hideous creature in disbelief, her back pressed against the door.

Extending its arms, the monster lunged for her throat. Acting quickly, she managed to slip away before its huge misshapen hands reached her neck.

Elizabeth, half mad with fear, dashed across the room. The creature followed her. She ran in circles, desperate to escape. Finally she found herself with her back to the door once more. The monster had her trapped! This time, as its hands reached out toward her neck, Elizabeth's voice returned. She let out a terrible shriek—a cry of utter hopelessness.

Frankenstein and Victor were in the cellar. They had already searched every corner of every room, with still no sign of the creature. Suddenly a high-pitched shriek cut through the musty cellar air.

"It's Elizabeth!" screamed Frankenstein. He dashed up the stairs, with Victor close at his heels. This is all my fault, Frankenstein thought as he ran. If anything happens to Elizabeth . . . But he could not complete this thought.

By the time Henry and Victor reached Elizabeth's room, the other guests at the party had gathered outside her door. Frankenstein frantically fumbled for the key to the bedroom, shoving his way through the crowd.

A crash came from behind the sealed door. The window, Henry thought. Someone's smashed the window!

Dr. Frankenstein finally found the right key. Then he turned the lock and threw open the door. The monster had crashed through the window and escaped when it heard the crowd gathering outside the door.

Frankenstein ran to Elizabeth, who was stretched out on her bed, unconscious. Her gown was tattered, evidence of her fight with the creature. Frankenstein kneeled by her side, fearing the worst.

"Elizabeth," he called anxiously. "Elizabeth!"

She stirred.

"Thank goodness, she's alive!" cried Frankenstein, relieved.

Elizabeth tossed her head back and forth, still in a state of shock. "Stop!" she moaned, raising her hands as if to push the creature away. "Leave me alone!"

"No, no, it's all right, darling," said Frankenstein. "Everything is going to be all right!"

Elizabeth looked up and recognized Henry. Then she closed her eyes and drifted back into unconsciousness.

Taking her hand, Henry gazed down at her, wondering if this dreadful ordeal would ever end.

CHAPTER 9
The Angry Mob

Outside in the streets the people of the village continued their celebration, unaware of the horrors occurring inside the Frankenstein villa.

As the townsfolk celebrated, Maria's father walked among them, his tear-stained, bloodshot eyes staring straight ahead, as if he were sleepwalking through some terrible nightmare.

Draped across his outstretched arms was the lifeless body of his beloved daughter.

He had returned home from his chores, planning to take Maria to the village for the celebration. He was looking forward to the time he would have with his daughter, away from the responsibilities of his work. He called out for her when he arrived back at their cabin. But there was no answer—only his own voice echoing thinly across the lake. Down at the shoreline, he spied something floating near the water's edge. He ran out into the water, splashing and crying, until he reached the limp body. It was too late!

Maria's father walked through the village, ignoring the party, for he had lost his whole world. Now he only sought revenge.

As he passed through the streets, the sounds of joy turned to gasps of horror. One by one the merrymakers nudged each other as they noticed his zombielike walk and the limp body of the little girl they all knew and loved. Women covered their faces with their hands, and men removed their hats. Children pointed and shouted "Look! It's Maria!" as the girl's father slowly, steadily made his way past them. Cries of fear and outrage replaced the festive music. The dancing stopped. Meals were abandoned, left half-finished. Windows swung open when those inside heard the woeful cries, and shocked villagers looked down on the scene below.

The crowd moved aside to let Maria's father pass. Then they closed in behind him. More and more people started to follow the grieving man, and the crowd became an outraged mob. Some villagers raised their voices in anger.

"It's murder!" shouted one.

"Find the killer!" screamed another.

"Let's get the Burgomaster!" yelled a third. "He'll help us find this brute!"

The seething mob, now moving very quickly, descended on the Burgomaster's home. The noise from the screaming crowd drifted up through the windows on the second floor. The Burgomaster threw open a window and saw the mob rushing up to his front door.

Police officers had to hold the crowd back, for they were attempting to break down the Burgomaster's door.

The Burgomaster threw on his coat and rushed onto the balcony. "Quiet!" he called to the unruly group. "Please, calm down!"

The roar slowly died away.

"What is it that brings you all here!" the Burgomaster asked. Then he looked down and saw Maria's body lying in her father's arms.

"It's Maria," sobbed her father, his voice cracking and his eyes red from crying. "She's dead!" His tears flowed freely now as he raised the body up for the Burgomaster to see.

The crowd started to roar once more, forcing the Burgomaster to ask again for silence.

"My poor man," he said sympathetically. "My heart goes out to you. But why do you bring her here to me?"

"She has been murdered!" cried the grieving father, anger beginning to cut through his tears.

The crowd surged forward.

"Find the murderer!" one man cried, and the others roared in agreement.

74

"Silence!" demanded the Burgomaster. "I will see that justice is done! Who has committed this terrible crime?"

"There is a fiend loose in the woods," explained a man who lived near the lake where Maria was found. "I saw someone, a very large man, out in the mountains."

"I saw him, too!" cried another. "A huge man, a beast!"

"Let's find this murderer!" shouted a third man, and the crowd shouted its approval.

"We will find him!" the Burgomaster said. "But first we must organize groups. Let's get started at once!"

Back in the villa, Victor was pacing the hallway outside Elizabeth's room. She was still in shock, but he knew she would be all right.

He was more concerned about Henry right then. Victor's friend had spent the rest of the day worrying and racked with guilt. Blaming himself for Elizabeth's condition, Henry appeared to have aged in just a few hours. He looked tired and drawn, and Victor was beginning to wonder whether he would ever recover from this horrible nightmare.

The door swung open, and Henry stepped out from Elizabeth's room.

"How is Elizabeth now?" Victor asked as soon as his friend had shut the door behind him.

"I don't know," replied Henry nervously, wringing his hands. "She's still in a daze. Oh, Victor, she just looks at me and says nothing. It's maddening!"

"Easy, Henry," said Victor, placing a comforting hand on his friend's shoulder. "She'll be all right!"

"Will she?" snapped Henry bitterly. "This was to have been our wedding day, and now . . ." He shuddered as his words trailed off.

"Steady," Victor said. "The wedding will only be postponed a day at most."

"A day?" said Henry, shaking his head. "I wonder."

"What do you mean?" Victor asked, not understanding.

"There can be no wedding while this horrible creation of mine is still alive!" Henry explained passionately. "I made it with these hands, and with these hands I will destroy it! I must find the monster!"

"I'll go with you," offered Victor.

"No!" Henry insisted. He moved closer to Victor and looked at him intently. "You stay here and look after Elizabeth. Whatever happens to me, I leave her in your care. Do you understand?"

Victor nodded silently as Henry rushed out into the gathering dusk. He stared after his friend for a moment, then continued his pacing outside Elizabeth's door.

Chapter 10
Fatal Fire

That night Henry joined the huge mob that had gathered outside the Burgomaster's home. The Burgomaster himself had spent the day organizing the crowd into three search parties. He had torches distributed, and hunting hounds brought around to aid them in their search for the monster.

Now he raised his hands, calling for quiet.

"Ludwig," he addressed Maria's father. "You will search the woods with your group." He turned toward Henry. "Dr. Frankenstein," he went on, "you take your people into the mountains. And I'll lead the third group to the lake."

The mob once again began to raise their voices in anger. Finally, the Burgomaster spoke.

"Remember!" he shouted. "Get the monster alive if you can, but get him in any case!"

A huge cry rose from the crowd.

"Search every ravine, every crevice!" he continued. "The fiend must be found!"

The crowd roared again.

"Are you ready?" asked the Burgomaster.

"Yes!" bellowed the crowd.

"Then light your torches," instructed the Burgomaster, "and let's get moving!"

The villagers lit their torches, then made their way through the village. The streets were filled with onlookers. Those who did not come out gazed down from their windows. The blood-red flare of the torches flickered across the spectators' faces as they watched the huge search party move through town. Women wept and prayed, holding their children close. Each one seemed to realize that the murdered child could easily have been her own.

Led by barking hounds, the mob headed toward the edge of town and the countryside that lay beyond. A short time later they reached the woods and split up into three groups. The Burgomaster took his men to the lake, where they boarded waiting rowboats. They floated off across the water, torches flaming, like an invading army.

Ludwig, Maria's father, led his group off into the woods. He was grateful that the whole town was behind him, but he also longed for his own, personal revenge. He wanted to destroy this monster himself.

Dr. Frankenstein led the third group up the mountain. The climb was not too difficult, and soon they reached the halfway point on their way to the top. There, the path split in two directions. Frankenstein divided up his party.

"You search there," he told half the group, pointing to the path on the left. "The rest of you come with me."

Frankenstein led his half up the rockier path, which led directly to the mountain's peak. After a few minutes of hard climbing, they reached a plateau. Frankenstein, in front of the others, spotted a man lying wounded on the ground, groaning in pain. He had been attacked by the monster only moments earlier!

"Up here!" Frankenstein called out to his group. "This way!" As the others arrived, he knelt down beside the injured man.

"Which way did the monster go?" asked Frankenstein.

The man propped himself up on one elbow and pointed toward the summit.

"You stay here and take care of this man," Frankenstein instructed a youth in his group. "The rest of you, follow me!"

A bugler sounded a signal before the men continued up the mountain.

Across the lake the Burgomaster and his people heard the call. It was clear that Frankenstein's group was hot on the creature's trail. The Burgomaster and his group hurried off to join them.

In the woods Ludwig also heard the call. Anxious to find the beast that had murdered his daughter, he quickly turned his group around and they headed toward the mountain as well.

All three groups now converged on that gray and brown mountain, which towered majestically against the moonlit sky.

The monster, silhouetted by the moonlight, stood on its very peak. Looking down, it saw the hostile mob and flaming torches slowly moving toward its hiding place. The creature wailed unhappily, then waved its arms, trying to make the people go away. Finally it crouched behind a large boulder and hid quietly.

Sensing that he was close to the creature, Dr. Frankenstein moved quickly. He felt responsible for every terrible thing that had occurred since he created his monster. Each incident lingered in his mind as he scrambled over the rocky terrain. The deaths of Fritz and Waldman, the attack on Elizabeth, and now the murder of an innocent child. All his fault! He moved like a man with a great purpose and was soon far ahead of his group.

Looking down from a high plateau, Frankenstein saw the others moving slowly up the mountain. He could see their torches and hear the dogs yelping as they struggled up the steep path.

"Come, this way!" he yelled. "Up here!" But he was too far away. Rather than wait for the others, Frankenstein set off on his own.

Far below, the others lost sight of the doctor. "Dr. Frankenstein, where are you?" they called up to him. But there was no answer. They continued to climb, angling away from Frankenstein and leaving him totally alone.

A few minutes later Dr. Frankenstein reached the summit. He didn't see the monster, who remained crouched behind a rock. Frankenstein, leaning over the edge of a cliff, waved his burning torch and called down to the others. No one answered. Then he turned around.

The creature, looking out from its hiding place, saw Frankenstein's face for the first time. Its mouth curled down in an expression of hatred, and its fear turned to anger.

It recognized this face. This was the first face it had ever seen. It didn't understand the connection, but somehow it knew that this man was the cause of all its pain and torment. This man was in some way responsible for its present predicament—trapped on a mountain ledge, pursued by an angry mob.

The monster stood up and stepped out from its hiding place, facing its creator.

Frankenstein, terrified, backed away frantically as the gigantic creature inched forward. The doctor was finally forced to stop when he reached a sheer rock wall and could retreat no farther. He hesitated for a moment, wondering what to do.

So this is how it ends, he thought. Just the creator and the creation. The doctor with the mad dreams alone with the product of those nightmares. Finally he stepped forward, thrusting the crimson torch before him, right at the monster's face.

But the monster, no longer afraid of fire, grabbed the torch from Frankenstein's hand and threw it to the ground. The doctor tried to dash past the creature, but he was not fast enough. The monster took him by the throat and began to shake his tall, thin body.

Below, on a small plateau, the group led by the Burgomaster met up with Ludwig's search party.

"Has anyone seen Dr. Frankenstein?" asked the Burgomaster.

Before anyone could answer, a cry of terror pierced the night.

"Help!" came the strangled plea.

"It's Dr. Frankenstein!" cried the Burgomaster.

"This way!" shouted Ludwig, pointing toward the mountain's peak.

There, silhouetted against the black sky, was a terrifying sight. The monster had Frankenstein in its grasp.

All the men in the search party hurried up the mountain.

At the summit the monster had just thrown

Frankenstein to the ground. The doctor got up and attacked the beast, hoping to knock it off balance. But the monster was ready for him. It clasped its huge hands together and swung them around like a mallet, striking Frankenstein in the mouth. The blow sent him crashing to the ground again. This time he was knocked unconscious. Blood trickled from the corner of his mouth.

Moments later the roar of the mob and the howling of the dogs came drifting up toward the monster. When it saw them approaching, it knew it had to flee. But it was not going to leave Frankenstein behind. It moved along the edge of the mountain, dragging the doctor's limp body behind it.

The monster looked around in panic, not knowing where to run for safety. Then it spotted an old abandoned windmill on the far side of the mountain, near its secondary peak. The building might provide some protection from the growling creatures, whose barking grew louder with each passing minute.

The monster slung Frankenstein over its shoulder and began running toward the mill. When it reached a large crevice in the rocks, it became momentarily visible to the Burgomaster below.

"Look, up there!" shouted the Burgomaster. "It's headed for the old windmill. Quick! Release the dogs!"

The leashes were unhooked, and the bloodhounds bolted up the rocks, heading for the mill.

The dilapidated wooden structure stood tall against the gathering clouds. Its vanes, hanging in shreds, had once turned majestically, milling grain for the whole village. Now these vanes were useless, and the mill was deserted.

The monster approached its huge oak front door just as the dogs appeared over the crest of the mountain. It knew that it had to get inside or it would be torn to pieces by the snarling hounds.

Using all of its considerable strength, the monster slammed its shoulder against the door, which creaked open slightly. Putting Frankenstein down, it used its powerful arms to shove the door all the way open. The monster picked up Frankenstein, dragged him inside, then slammed the door shut just as the hounds reached the mill. They barked and growled at the great wooden door, leaping up against it, but they were locked outside. The monster was safe for the moment.

Still carrying Frankenstein, the monster moved across the small circular room that formed the mill's ground floor. Then it went up a rickety old stairway that led to a trapdoor in the ceiling. Supporting Frankenstein with one arm, it pushed the trapdoor open with the other.

The trapdoor landed with a thud, sending out dust and splinters. The monster pulled itself through the opening, then stood there, looking around. Dropping

Frankenstein's unconscious body to the floor, the creature peered out a second-story window. Below, the lights of the torches revealed the mob climbing toward the mill.

The monster roared in fear and panic. Picking Frankenstein up and slinging him back over its shoulder, the creature made its way up a shaky ladder to the top floor of the mill. As it dumped Frankenstein's body onto the filthy wooden floor, it heard a crash at the front door.

The villagers, using a huge log as a battering ram, were bashing the sturdy oak door over and over again.

On the top floor of the mill, Frankenstein suddenly came to. His head ached, his body was sore, and he was momentarily confused. Where was he, he wondered, and what was going on?

As soon as he spotted the monster across the room, he realized he must have been dragged to this place—wherever it was! He thought for a moment, knowing he had to find a way to escape. Then he slowly crawled across the damp floor. He was almost at the ladder when his foot accidentally knocked against an old toolbox.

The monster spun around at the sound. Growling menacingly, it ran across the circular room just as the doctor sprang to his feet.

The two foes circled each other warily. Frankenstein

managed to keep the monster at bay, but he knew that his time was running out.

Suddenly another crash from the battering ram sounded downstairs at the front door. It caught the monster's attention. This was the chance Frankenstein was looking for. He dashed past the distracted creature, rushing out onto the balcony. Below him the mob had gathered. It was a long way down, but he had to take the risk.

Frankenstein threw one leg over the balcony railing. He was hoping to reach out and grab one of the old vanes of the windmill and lower himself down from there. A shout went up from the crowd below when they caught sight of him.

As he lifted his other leg to clear the rail, he felt a hand close, viselike, on his ankle. The monster was upon him, pulling him back over the railing and tossing him down to the balcony floor.

"There it is!" shouted the Burgomaster when he saw the monster on the balcony. "The murderer!"

The monster fell on top of Frankenstein, its crushing weight momentarily knocking the wind out of the doctor. The two grappled on the balcony floor, wrestling in a life-or-death struggle.

Using all of its strength, the exhausted monster threw Frankenstein off its body, sending him rolling under the balcony's guard rail. The crowd below gasped in horror as they saw the doctor's body tumbling down.

FRANKENSTEIN

But Frankenstein's fall was broken by one of the windmill's old vanes. His weight caused the vane to turn, gently lowering him down. He slipped off the vane at its lowest point and hit the ground with a dull thud.

A crowd quickly formed around Frankenstein, who lay motionless on the ground. "Dr. Frankenstein!" the Burgomaster called. "Dr. Frankenstein!" He bent over and discovered that Frankenstein was still alive.

"Take him down to the village," the Burgomaster ordered a few of his men. "See that he gets immediate medical attention!"

The men carefully lifted Frankenstein and began carrying him down the mountain, away from this horrible scene.

"The fiend is still alive!" screamed a villager, spotting the monster still standing on the balcony.

"Burn the mill!" shouted another man.

The crowd grew excited. "Yes, burn the mill!" they cried.

The villagers abandoned their battering ram and grabbed their flaming torches. One by one, dozens of angry villagers placed their torches at the bottom of the mill.

The monster peered down from the balcony and let out a pitiful wail. It was trapped, with no chance of escape.

The monster waved its arms frantically. It lifted an

old wooden crate high above its head and prepared to throw it off the balcony, onto the crowd below.

But it was too late. One of the vanes had already caught fire. A strong gust of wind caused the vane to turn, bringing it, burning, up to the level of the balcony.

The monster dropped the crate and screamed in terror as the balcony's railing burst into flame.

The terrified creature retreated back into the mill. Outside, the lower portion of the building was now completely engulfed in fire. Then the burning balcony set the third floor ablaze. The monster had nowhere to hide.

The creature's shrieks could be heard by the crowd below. The burning vane crashed to the ground, followed by a piece of the mill's roof. The villagers cheered as sections of the flaming structure came tumbling down.

And then the monster's mournful cries stopped.

All that could be heard now was the crackling of burning wood. The orange flames lit up the sky, and the villagers knew the creature was gone.

Epilogue

The sun rose on a new day—the first peaceful day Dr. Henry Frankenstein had seen in several months.

After Frankenstein's escape from the creature, the villagers had carried him down the mountain and back to his home. A doctor was then summoned. Fortunately, Frankenstein had only received a few bruises in his fall, but he was totally exhausted by his ordeal, and the doctor prescribed several days of bed rest. Following this, the doctor said, Frankenstein would be as good as new, and his wedding could take place at any time.

Henry was now resting comfortably in his bed at the villa. Elizabeth sat in a chair by his side. She had already recovered from her encounter with the monster, and she was now relieved to find her Henry getting better every day.

She held his hand as he slept, watching the peaceful expression on his face. Her mind was filled with thoughts of their wedding, which was finally going to take place.

Henry's father, Baron Frankenstein, was also in the room. Today he was a happy man. After the horrible things they had all been through, a sense of calm and order was returning to the Frankenstein villa. Nothing could have pleased the Baron more.

Just then there was a knock on the door. Baron Frankenstein got up to answer it.

Several of the servants were gathered in the hallway outside Henry's bedroom. One of them carried three glasses and a bottle of wine on a silver tray.

"Well, well, well," the Baron said, looking curiously at the servants. "What's all this about? What do you want, eh?" He walked out into the hallway, closing the door behind him.

"If you please, Baron," began the servant holding the tray. "We thought Mr. Henry could do with a glass of his great-grandmother's wine."

"Fine old woman, my grandmother," mumbled the Baron. "Very thoughtful of her to prevent my grandfather from drinking this. Now I get to enjoy it!"

The servants laughed at the Baron's joke.

"Henry doesn't need this now," the Baron explained. "He just needs to rest. I'll have some, though, and I'd like to make one more toast."

The servant poured out a glass, which the Baron lifted high into the air. "I've said this before, but I'll say it again. Here's a wish for a happy marriage, and a long life for Henry and Elizabeth!"

"Indeed, sir," said a servant. "We hope so as well!"

The Baron sipped the fine wine, confident now that his wish had an excellent chance of coming true.